HONKERS

by Jane Yolen
Illustrated by Leslie Baker

Little, Brown and Company
Boston   Toronto   London

Also by Jane Yolen and Leslie Baker
All Those Secrets of the World

Text copyright © 1993 by Jane Yolen
Illustrations copyright © 1993 by Leslie Baker

First Edition

Library of Congress Cataloging-in-Publication Data

Yolen, Jane.
    Honkers / by Jane Yolen ; illustrated by Leslie Baker. — 1st ed.
      p.   cm.
    Summary: While staying at her grandparents' farm until the birth
of her mother's baby, homesick Betsy learns a lesson about
independence when she witnesses the birth and migration of a
gosling.
    ISBN 0-316-96893-5
    [1. Geese — Fiction. 2. Homesickness — Fiction. 3. Birth — Fiction.
4. Farm life — Fiction.] I. Baker, Leslie A., ill. II. Title.
PZ7.Y78Hr   1993
[E] — dc20   92-24302

10 9 8 7 6 5 4 3 2

BER

Published simultaneously in Canada
by Little, Brown & Company (Canada) Limited
Printed in the United States of America

Paintings done in watercolor on Strathmore Bristol

For my children, Heidi, Adam, and Jason,
who watch birds,
and in memory of Heidi's silky blanket,
which she carried off with her to college
— J. Y.

For Ann
— L. B.

IT WAS THE MIDDLE OF SPRING, the trees all hazy, and the wild geese flew overhead in long noisy vees going north.

Betsy's mama was having a hard time waiting for the birth of her new baby and had to stay long, boring hours in bed. Betsy's daddy was too hard at work to take care of her.

"Send her to us at the farm," wrote Nana. "There's room enough and more."

So Betsy was packed off with a trunk full of clothes, three reading books, and her silky blanket, the one she'd had forever. At the train station, Daddy tied a tag with her name on it through her buttonhole.

"Special delivery," he said and winked at the conductor. Then he waved and waved as the train pulled out, until he was so small, Betsy couldn't see his hand from his jacket, his jacket from the station, the station from the rest of the town. She clutched the silky blanket, but she would not cry. Crying was for babies; she was Daddy's big girl now.

Grandy, in his green peaked cap, met the train. "Welcome back, Little Bit," he said, his voice full of smiles.

"Betsy," she reminded him.

"You bet," he said.

At the farm, Nana hugged her twice over, once for love and once for luck. Betsy always missed Nana when she was home, but suddenly she missed home more. She held the silky tighter to keep from crying.

"There's a surprise waiting in the barn," Nana said.

Betsy ran off without even unpacking, the silky flapping behind her like a cape.

In the cool, hay-scented barn, a nest made of flannels held three large glossy white eggs.

"Honkers," Grandy said. "Found 'em down by the river a few days ago."

"Abandoned, poor little mites," Nana added. "Off in the world on their own. We thought we'd raise them, seeing there's room enough and more."

Betsy touched the eggs: one, then the next, then the next.

"Choose," said Grandy.

Betsy looked carefully, then pointed at the middle one. Grandy took a blue pen and made a small B on the side of the egg.

"Will it hatch?" Betsy asked.

"When it's ready," Grandy said.

"And God willing," added Nana.

They went for a walk down the dirt road that stretched between the house and a cattail pond. Betsy put her arms up like wings, running on ahead and calling, "*Uh-whonk, uh-whonk, uh-whonk!*"

Grandy laughed and slapped his thigh. "By golly, a honker! Look at 'er fly!"

Betsy stopped and closed her eyes. If she had been a *real* honker, she would have flown right back to her own house — if she had only known the way.

Betsy turned the eggs twice a day, the way Grandy showed her.

"Keeps the heat in," he said. "Keeps the eggs from sticking to the insides of the shells."

She turned them all, expecting the eggs to get bigger and bigger, like Mama with the baby inside. But they never seemed to grow. After a while, the blue *B* was almost rubbed off of her egg.

"Should take twenty-five days altogether," said Nana. "Lots faster than a baby sister or brother."

Betsy thought of Mama at home, lying on her brass bed. "Twenty-five days sounds plenty long enough to me."

Those days went by quick and slow. Quick and slow. Quick when letters came written in Mama's careful hand. But so slow in between. Betsy kept the silky close at night.

And then came the pearly day the eggs cracked.

Betsy saw a little z like lightning on her own egg first. It ran right across the blue smudge.

"Starting!" Grandy said with a satisfied grunt.

"Takes time," Nana added.

Betsy spread the silky on the hay beside the flannel nest and settled down on it to wait.

She watched all that day. Nana brought out lunch. Grandy brought out lemonade and his harmonica. They played Checkers and Spit-in-the-Ocean, sitting on the hay.

The z on the egg grew longer. Betsy could hear a wild peeping coming from inside the shell, high and frantic.

"Maybe we should break the eggs open, Grandy," she said.

He shook his head. "Mother Nature is sometimes hard on things. And not always fair. But she doesn't like to be rushed. Not even by a little bit."

"Betsy," Betsy said.

"Not even by her," he agreed.

That night Betsy slept in the barn. Nana slept beside her. Grandy grumbled and said he was too old for that sort of camping out. "Honkers never hatch at night," he said.

He went off to bed in the house but left on all the lights.

"In case you need to find the way," he said.

The sun was just rising when the first gosling pecked its way out. Pieces of the blue-smudged shell stuck to its wet back. Its dark eyes were wide.

"Hi, Little Bit," Betsy whispered. She picked the gosling up and put it beside her on the silky.

"*Peep, peep,*" it said.

An hour later, when Nana was awake, the other two goslings hatched out. As soon as their down dried, no one could tell them apart. But Little Bit followed Betsy all around the barn.

Grandy came out with a tin tub filled with water. Betsy made a ramp up to it out of a wooden plank. While the goslings took their first swim, she put hay around the outside of the tub as high as its rim, and the silky blanket on top of the hay.

"This is your home now, Little Bit," Betsy said. "Just like it's mine. And I am your new mama."

At the sound of her voice, all three of the goslings looked up. "*Peep, peep, peep,*" they said.

The goslings grew and grew. In a week, they were two times bigger, just like the pile of Mama's letters. Betsy kept the letters in a wooden box. The geese soon grew too big for the tin tub.

"Those geese are like little mounds of butter," Nana said.

"Like eating machines," grumbled Grandy.

The goslings followed Betsy everywhere: to the barn, to the pond, to the house, even up on the porch. When she went in for lunch and they couldn't see her through the window, they would cry, *"Oh!oo, oh!oo"* so loudly, she'd have to come right out.

"There, there," she'd say. "Don't worry. I haven't forgotten you." And they'd make a sound like someone chuckling: *"Wheeoo-wheeoo."*

"Spoiled rotten," said Grandy.

In the middle of the summer, they took to grazing in Nana's garden.

"Shoo!" Nana would cry, running out after them and flapping her apron. "Shoo!" But they wouldn't go away. "Betsy, I need help."

But even Betsy couldn't scare them off.

Finally Grandy came out with Nana's big red umbrella. He sneaked up on them and — *swooooosh-pop!* — opened the umbrella.

The three geese rose up into the air on their wide new wings and flew right to the cattail pond.

"You're in charge now," Grandy said, handing the umbrella to Betsy. "You're plenty big enough to keep those geese out of Nana's vegetables."

"Almost six," Betsy answered.

"You bet," he said.

By summer's end, Mama's letters had to be kept in two wooden boxes. The geese were full grown, standing as high as Betsy's shoulder, their cheek patches gleaming white. They spent most days at the pond eating weeds and mustard grass and preening their feathers. But they still came back each night to sleep on the silky.

"What will they do when I go home?" Betsy asked. Mama's latest letter had said it would be soon.

Grandy was silent for a long moment. Then he raised his head and sniffed the wind. "Smell that," he said. "Fall's on the way."

Betsy sniffed. She could smell the hay in the barn and new-mown grass. She could smell cookies cooling on the porch. And something more, something crisp like apples when you first bite down.

"That's the smell of fall, and those geese will be flying off soon."

"Where will they go?"

"South," he said. "Home."

"But *this* is home."

"Not forever."

"How will they know the way?"

Grandy smiled and put his arm around her. "The heart has its own compass, Betsy, girl. They'll know."

One day soon after, Betsy heard a great noise overhead.

"Honkers, by golly!" said Grandy, looking up.

Little Bit stretched her neck, listening. Her brother and sister began to run across the yard — one step, two. Then they leapt into the air. Flapping their wings, they sped upward toward the sound.

Little Bit walked over to Betsy and shoved her beak under Betsy's arm.

"She wants you to fly," said Nana. "She wants you flying home with her."

"I *am* going home," Betsy whispered. "Tomorrow. But not that way." She pushed Little Bit from her.

Little Bit gave one soft "*Oh!oo*," then ran a step and was gone into the air, her wings pumping hard.

Betsy watched her circle the house and barn. She could see the goose's cheek patch until it got so small, she couldn't tell the patch from the head, the head from the body, the goose from the bright sky.

Betsy cried all that night. Nana did, too. The one time Grandy came to check on Betsy, she could see patches on his cheeks like Little Bit's, only his were red instead of white.

The next day Grandy and Nana took her to the train so she could ride home, where Mama and Daddy and her new sister waited. The tag with her name and address was tied through the buttonhole of her coat. The reading books lay unread in her lap. She'd left the silky behind in the barn.

Out the window, the land rushed by. Sometimes Betsy could see color changing on the trees. Sometimes she could see the wind moving the leaves. But mostly she watched the geese through the glass; the long noisy vees. They were going south, just as she was, following the compasses of their hearts home.